Alfred Nobel

Alfred Nobel

INVENTIVE THINKER

TRISTAN BOYER BINNS

BPMS MEDIA CENTER

FRANKLIN WATTS
A Division of Scholastic Inc.
New York Toronto London Auckland Sydney
Mexico City New Delhi Hong Kong
Danbury, Connecticut

To Andy, for giving me both the hurdles and the means to jump over them.

ACKNOWLEDGMENTS

The author would like to thank the following sources for permission to reproduce copyrighted material:

Thomas A. Edison Papers, Rutgers University (Chapter Four)

Extract from Henry du Pont letter, courtesy of Hagley Museum and Library (Chapter Four)

Albert Einstein Archives, Jewish National & University Library, Hebrew University of Jerusalem (Chapter Eleven)

Extract from THE LEGACY OF ALFRED NOBEL by Ragnar Sohlman published by Bodley Head.
Used by permission of The Random House Group Limited. Permission also given by The Nobel Foundation.
(Chapters Ten and Eleven)

Photographs © 2004: AKG-Images, London: 15 (St. Petersburg, State Hermitage), back cover; AP/Wide World Photos/Dave Caulkin: 98; Bridgeman Art Library International Ltd., London/New York: 12 (Nationalmuseum, Stockholm, Sweden), 59 (Private Collection); Brown Brothers: 51, 64; Corbis Images: 46 (Ed Eckstein), 21 (Hulton-Deutsch Collection), 18 (Gianni Dagli Orti), 53 (Leonard de Selva); Fundamental Photos, New York/Jeff J. Daly: 26; Mary Evans Picture Library: 8, 10, 30, 70, 74 top, 74 bottom; The Nobel Foundation: cover, 2, 6, 9, 16, 22, 32, 34, 36, 38, 40, 41, 48, 54, 56, 60, 72, 76, 77, 79, 84, 87, 89, 94.

Library of Congress Cataloging-in-Publication Data

Binns, Tristan Boyer, 1968–
   Alfred Nobel / Tristan Boyer Binns.
     p. cm. — (Great life stories)

Summary: Discusses the life and work of Alfred Nobel, a Swedish inventor who developed dynamite and instituted the Nobel Prize.

Includes bibliographical references and index.

ISBN 0-531-12328-6

1. Nobel, Alfred Bernhard, 1833–1896—Juvenile literature. 2. Chemical engineers—Sweden—Biography—Juvenile literature. 3. Philanthropists—Sweden—Biography—Juvenile literature. [1. Nobel, Alfred Bernhard, 1833–1896. 2. Chemical engineers. 3. Scientists. 4. Nobel Prizes—History.] I. Title. II. Series.

TP268.5.N7B56 2004
660'.092—dc22

2003013349

Contents

Nobel was born in a house on this street in Stockholm.

Childhood and Family

On October 21, 1833, a boy named Alfred Nobel was born in a small house in Stockholm, Sweden. He would become an important inventor and world figure. During his lifetime, he changed the world through his invention of explosives such as dynamite. Dynamite made possible the major industrial and transportation growth that built up the United States and made Europe even stronger. Since his death, Nobel has been remembered for the Nobel Prizes awarded each year to people who have also made their marks on the world in an important way.

At first, Alfred was a weak baby who had to struggle to live. His mother, Andriette, cared fiercely for Alfred, helping him grow strong enough to survive. The household was poor. In 1832, the family's house had burned down. Most of their furniture and the things they owned had burned in the fire. The apartment Alfred was born in was cold and drafty. Sometimes his older brothers, Robert and Ludvig, had to sell matches on the street to earn money to buy food.

Alfred's fortune would change during his life. Despite his penniless beginning, he became one of the richest men in Europe. Being born poor may have encouraged him to work very hard. He also grew up in a family of curious, technically minded people. They met some big obstacles, but were good problem solvers who found ways to turn bad fortune into useful learning experiences. Although Alfred was never outwardly proud of his life and his abilities, he could turn most setbacks into opportunities. He hardly ever rested, despite being ill most of his life. He was the happiest he ever became when working around the clock solving a new problem.

FAMILY HISTORY

One of Alfred Nobel's great-great-great grandfathers was a famous Swede, Olof Rudbeck, who lived from 1630 to 1702. Rudbeck was famous for discovering how a part of the

Olof Rudbeck was a famous Swede. He was a very capable thinker in many fields.

human body called the lymphatic system works. He was a writer and an artist as well as a scientist. He wrote a long book of philosophy and history called *Atlantica*.

Alfred's great-great grandfather was the first in his family to take the name Nobel. In the late 1600s, people usually stayed in the areas in which they were born. If they left, they often made that place name into their last name. When Peder Olufsson, who lived from 1655 to 1707, left his home in the Swedish area of Östra Nöbbelöv to go to Uppsala University in 1682, he changed his name to Petrus Olai Nobelius. That is the Latin way of saying the Swedish name Peder Östra Nöbbelöv. Alfred's grandfather Immanuel was born in 1757. He shortened his last name from Nobelius to Nobell, then to Nobel.

Alfred's father, Immanuel, was born on March 24, 1801. His parents, Immanuel and Brita, were poor. After receiving a basic education, the young Immanuel became a sailor for three years. He then returned to Sweden and started working with a builder in Gävle. In those days, all building plans had to be drawn by hand.

Immanuel Nobel worked on many projects during his life. He is best remembered as Alfred's father, but he also developed exploding underwater mines and invented plywood.

Accuracy and imagination were necessary for making plans that were clear enough to be followed by builders. Immanuel studied architecture. He learned to draw well and won prizes for his plans for a portable house and a spiral staircase.

Immanuel was skilled at solving building problems and got many jobs constructing and fixing buildings. He was only twenty-four years old when he started inventing machines and applying for patents. When he married Andriette Ahlsell in 1827, he was inventing ways to make building tools, surgical instruments, and floating rubber mattresses. The family was doing well and looked forward to a happy future. Alfred's brother Robert was born in 1829, and Ludvig was born in 1831. Then the family members lost almost everything they had in a string of accidents. A barge sank and took many of Immanuel's building materials with it, a project he was working on went wrong, and their house burned down. By January 1833, the family was bankrupt.

Andriette Nobel came from a family that had more money than Immanuel's, but she seldom asked for help even when the Nobels were at the bottom of their fortunes. Alfred was devoted to her throughout his whole life.

Sickness and Death

When Alfred Nobel was young, more people died than were born each year in Sweden. People often got sick with diseases that were passed along to many others because the water wasn't clean and there was no good way to get rid of garbage and human waste. There weren't any flushing toilets connected to sewers. People used outhouses in backyards instead. Because so many people got sick in these epidemics, many children died while they were young.

FROM DISASTER TO SUCCESS

Andriette looked after Alfred and his two older brothers, Robert and Ludvig. She worked hard to make clothing for the family, cook what food they had, and keep everyone healthy. Andriette and Immanuel had six children, but only four lived to become adults. Alfred was sickly throughout his life, but he lived to be sixty-three years old.

Immanuel kept working as an inventor and builder, earning just enough money for the family to live on. He was very interested in rubber. Factories in those days were often very small because mass production was rare. In 1835, Immanuel opened Sweden's first factory that manufactured products made of rubber, such as surgical instruments and elastic cloth. He was working to perfect mines that contained rubber. He tried to sell the government of Sweden on the idea of mines that could be used on land or in the sea to protect the country from invaders, but the government was not interested in his ideas.

By 1837, Immanuel was still having problems because of his bankruptcy. In those days, people had to pay off the debts that had driven them to bankruptcy. If they couldn't, they might be sent to a special prison called debtors' prison. This was a harsh punishment. Being in prison made it very difficult ever to repay the debts. Immanuel was threatened with a sentence requiring a stay in debtors' prison. At a party, he met a man who worked for the government in Finland. This man was interested in Immanuel's mines. He asked Immanuel to go to Finland. Immanuel decided to go and see if he could make more money there and escape the threat of prison in Sweden. Andriette and the three boys stayed in Stockholm.

Andriette's father was an accountant. Her family was fairly successful and stayed close to the Nobels during their hard years. When Immanuel left for Finland, Andriette's father gave her enough money to survive and to open a small grocery store near their home. She worked alone and worked hard, selling milk and vegetables.

Robert, Ludvig, and Alfred went to the Jacob Parish Apologist School. Each child started school when he turned seven. The school was rough. The other students were also from poor families. One student

In 1835, Stockholm was a bustling, modern city. Like most cities at the time, the rich areas were beautiful and the poorer areas were often squalid and disease ridden.

who went to the school before the Nobels did said the students fought each other in and out of school. The students also got beaten by instructors for making mistakes in class. The teachers thought that if children were afraid to make mistakes, they would make fewer of them.

Alfred had a hard time in school. He was not a healthy child, so he couldn't keep up with his rough classmates. He was often sick for long periods of time. Throughout his life, he suffered from infected sinuses, bad headaches, and upset stomachs. When he was eighteen years old, he wrote a poem in English about his life, which told the story of his childhood in his own words.

> My cradle looked a deathbed, and for years
> a mother watched with ever anxious care,
> so little chance, to save the flickering light,
>
> We find him now a boy. His weakness still
> makes him a stranger in the little world,
> wherein he moves. When fellow boys are playing
> he joins them not, a pensive looker-on

Even though Alfred had a hard time, he learned quickly. His grades were very good. He earned high marks in the subjects the students were graded on, "Power of Comprehension," "Industriousness," and "Manners." This means he thought clearly, worked hard, and knew how to behave.

While Andriette and her three sons were doing their best to survive in Stockholm, Immanuel was working hard. He spent a few years in Turku, Finland, working on his mine experiments. He earned money working as an architect and builder. In about 1840, he moved to St. Petersburg, Russia, to work with industrial machinery. Immanuel worked to convince the Russian government that his land and sea mines would be helpful in defending the country. At the same time, he started a company that made tools, central heating pipes, gun carriages, and machines that manufactured wagon wheels. By 1842, he had enough money saved to bring his family to Russia to join him.

THE FAMILY IN ST. PETERSBURG

The Nobels sailed for St. Petersburg in October 1842. The house they moved into was nicer than their home in Stockholm. St. Petersburg itself was a city of palaces, bridges, and impressive roads on the Neva River. It was a great city of the time, bustling with activity. Scientists were working on important new discoveries. People attended operas, concerts, and exhibitions of artwork. It is not known what the Nobels thought when they first arrived in St. Petersburg. Another Swedish immigrant, the

Why Finland?

The connection between Finland, Sweden, and Russia was strong during this era. Finland had been ruled by the Swedish king until 1809, when the Russians took over the country. From 1809 to 1917, the country was called the Grand Duchy of Finland. It was ruled by the Russian czar, who lived St. Petersburg. Even though it was controlled by another country, Finland had its own laws and constitution.

nurse Maja Huss, wrote what she saw in the city. "The Neva is a splendid, beautiful wide river, with kilometer-long bridges crossing it. There is palace after palace. . . ."

In 1843, Alfred's brother Emil was born. As Immanuel's success increased, he became very well known as one of the best engineers in Russia. He paid off his debts in Sweden and the Nobels moved into a series of nicer houses and even had a summer home.

The whole time they lived in St. Petersburg, Robert, Ludvig, and Alfred Nobel had private tutors. They learned chemistry, mathematics, and physics from two Russian professors, Nikolai Zinin and Yuli Trapp. They learned history, languages, and philosophy from a Swedish teacher, Lars Santesson. Alfred worked very hard and mastered many subjects. He studied English literature and learned Russian, German, French, and English.

Alfred had spent only two years in school and didn't stay in touch with any friends from Stockholm. By the time he was seventeen years old, he had done most of his studies working only with his brothers. He didn't have friends beyond his family and his teachers. Alfred liked to

St. Petersburg was an industrial and social center, filled with examples of great classical architecture. This painting shows Nevsky Prospect, one of the main avenues in the city.

spend time alone, thinking, reading, and experimenting. He pushed himself to work hard. He had a very good memory and could reason and think clearly. Alfred was still often sick with headaches and upset stomachs.

Immanuel and the boys were always learning, working together, and solving problems. Immanuel thought that knowledge was very important, but also thought that science was the most important kind of knowledge. He wrote a letter to his brother-in-law, Ludvig Ahlsell, saying, ". . . my good and industrious Alfred is highly valued both by his parents and his brothers for his knowledge as well as for his untiring work ability, which nothing can replace." When Alfred was seventeen years old, in 1850, he seemed to want to become a writer. His father thought this was not a serious profession. In order to dissuade Alfred from this career, Immanuel sent him on a two-year trip to study chemistry and engineering.

This photo of Alfred (on the left) and Ludvig was taken around 1850. Even teenagers in the 1800s wore formal suits.

Explosives and Experiments

Alfred Nobel left St. Petersburg for Sweden in the summer of 1850. He spent the summer in Dalarö, Sweden, with his uncle, Ludvig Ahlsell, and his cousins. Historians think that Nobel then went to Germany and Italy, meeting business contacts of his father. He spent some time in Paris with Professor Jules Pelouze to study chemistry.

In Paris, Nobel first heard about nitroglycerin (spelled nitroglycerine in Europe), the explosive that was to make his fortune. It would still be a few years, however, before he would understand how it worked. Paris is also where Nobel fell in love for the first time with a Swedish girl he met there. He wrote a letter about this experience.

I came to Paris—an ocean where Passion creates stormy weather and causes more wrecks than ever the salty waves did. . . . My life, before then a desolate desert, came alive in felicity and hope. I had a goal, a heavenly goal: to win this lovely girl and be worthy of her. I felt infinite happiness and we met again, and again and again, until we had become each other's heaven . . .

The girl died from tuberculosis while Nobel was still in Paris. Nobel was miserable and decided to dedicate his life to noble pursuits instead of "the pleasures of the masses." Maybe this sad experience was the reason Alfred Nobel never married or had children.

Paris in 1850 was full of fashionable cafés where people met to talk. Alfred Nobel probably enjoyed the parks and cafés while he visited there.

After leaving Paris, it seems Nobel went to the United States. His father Immanuel wanted him to meet the engineer John Ericsson, who was also Swedish. At the time, the Nobels were doing a great deal of work to improve central heating systems. Steam was used in central heating as well as to drive engines. Immanuel Nobel was working on a way to use heated air instead of steam to heat buildings. His friend Ericsson was an expert on using heated air to drive engines. Alfred Nobel went to New York to learn as much as possible about heated air and these engines from their inventor. He wanted to see how to apply Ericsson's ideas to the Nobels' central heating systems.

THE CRIMEAN WAR CHANGES THINGS

Alfred Nobel traveled back to St. Petersburg in July 1852 and went straight to work for his father's business. Robert and Ludvig already

John Ericsson

John Ericsson was born in Sweden in 1803, but moved to London in 1826 and then to the United States in 1839. Like many other inventors, he felt that Sweden didn't offer enough opportunity for him to develop his ideas. Ericsson made an engine that was powered by heated air. He also worked on ships, improving the design of the screw propeller. He is best known for the ship he designed for the Union side during the American Civil War. The *Monitor* was plated with iron. It fought the Confederate ship *Merrimac* during the Battle of Hampton Roads in 1862.

worked in it. As general engineers and scientists, they had to determine what needed to be made and then figure out how to make it. They took raw materials and turned them into finished items with the help of machine tools. Most of their products were metal goods, such as steam engines and pipes for plumbing and heating. Alfred Nobel worked very hard, especially when the Crimean War began in 1853. The Nobel company grew larger and changed its name to Nobel and Sons. The company was very busy with war materials. Immanuel designed rapid-firing rifles and the company manufactured them for the Russian army. The company also made guns, propellers, and engine parts for the Russian navy's ships.

The Russian government was now very interested in Immanuel's sea mines. They were laid in ports in Finland and near St. Petersburg. Robert oversaw the laying of the mines. Although no enemy ships hit the mines, one exploded and killed a man when it was brought on board the English ship *Duke of Wellington*. A Russian ship hit a mine and was badly damaged near a group of English ships. After this, the English were afraid of the mines. Admiral Napier, who led the English and French attacking forces, was frightened off by the mines. He wrote to his commanders that "the Gulf of Finland is full of infernal machines."

Alfred Nobel worked so hard that he needed a complete rest during the summer of 1854. He went to Dalarö in Sweden to visit his uncle and cousins again, and then to the spa at Franzenbad in the present-day Czech Republic near Germany. It was popular to rest and "take the cure" by swimming in spa water and drinking a great deal of it too, which often tasted terrible. Unlike today's spas, there was little exercise or pampering at Franzenland. Nobel was bored by the cure, and kept

The Crimean War

In 1850, Turkey controlled much of the Middle East. Russia and France were disagreeing with Turkey over the way Christians were being treated in the Middle East. Russia and France were also disagreeing with each other over what rights different Christian groups should have in Palestine, which Christians, Jews, and Muslims all consider a holy part of the world. When Turkey sided with the British and French, Russia got very upset and invaded Moldavia and Wallachia (in present-day Romania). The Crimean War began in 1853 when Turkey declared war on Russia. When the war ended with the signing of the Treaty of Paris in 1856, Russia fared poorly in all the complicated agreements and felt humiliated.

working while he was there. He wrote home, "It is easy to see how much you lose when you trade relatives and friends for temporary acquaintances with whom you can spend some pleasant hours, but with whom you can part, feeling about as much loss as you would for an old coat." Throughout his life, he never liked making casual acquaintances or wasting his time by not being involved completely in work.

RUINED AGAIN

When the Crimean War ended in 1856, a new government took over Russia. The new leaders didn't honor the agreements the former government had made. Suddenly, Nobel and Sons' work dried up. The money Immanuel had borrowed to expand the company had to be repaid. In 1858, he sent Alfred Nobel to Paris and London to ask the bankers there to loan them more money. The bankers refused, and Immanuel went bankrupt again.

Alfred Nobel was a young man during the Crimean War. He was in his early twenties when it ended, and he had to help try to his family's business afloat.

Immanuel, Andriette, and Emil moved back to Sweden in 1859. Robert, Ludvig, and Alfred stayed in St. Petersburg and did what they could to save the family's finances. They worked to pay back their debts and start over. Ludvig took over the running of the company. He sold what he could and sent enough money back to Sweden to help his parents settle there. Ludvig had married his cousin, Mina Ahlsell, in 1858. Their first son, Emanuel, was born in 1859. When the original Nobel company was sold, Ludvig started a company of his own in 1862 in St. Petersburg. It made weapons and industrial tools, such as rock drills and steam hammers.

Robert and Alfred Nobel lived in a small apartment. Alfred spent his time doing experiments in the kitchen. Then Robert married a Finnish woman named Pauline Lenngren and moved to Helsingfors, Finland, with her in 1862. Robert started a company that made bricks, and also founded the Aurora Lamp Oil Company around 1863. He sold lamps and the oil to burn in them. The business did not do well, but Robert learned a great deal about buying, selling, and refining oil.

THREE

Early Nitroglycerin

Most of the success the Nobels had came because they made things people needed, such as building materials and engines. They knew a great deal about how building projects were carried out. They had some success with Immanuel's mines and rifles, but they were known more for their central heating systems than their explosives. This was about to change.

By the 1860s, society was changing. People were traveling more and using more goods. Goods, such as fabric, that used to be handmade were now mass produced on machines made of metal and powered by coal. This made them cheaper and more widely available. The steam trains that traveled the new railroad tracks were powered by coal, and the tracks they rolled on were made of metal. People were amazed by the great engineering works that were going on, including the creation of railways and the building of huge bridges. These changes relied on an explosive called gunpowder. It was used to blast the mines and quarries from which coal and the raw materials used to make metals were extracted. It was also used to blast away the rock in the path of the bridges and tunnels.

No one knows for sure when gunpowder was first invented, but it was probably around the 1100s in China. Gunpowder is a mixture of saltpeter (or potassium nitrate), charcoal, and sulfur. Once it is lit, it will keep burning even without air because the saltpeter makes oxygen as it burns. Gunpowder creates hot gas quickly when it is burned, and the hot gas creates pressure. If a container such as a hollow cannonball is filled with gunpowder, the pressure produced when the gunpowder burns will blow the container apart. The pressure can also be used to force a bullet out of a gun barrel or to blast solid rock into gravel.

The problem with gunpowder is that it isn't very efficient. A lot of it is needed to blow things up. As industry's needs grew, a more efficient explosive was needed. Also, when gunpowder was used in cannon and

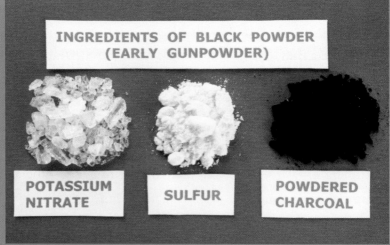

For centuries gunpowder was the best explosive anyone had invented. It is made up of these chemicals, and looks black when mixed. Sometimes it was called black powder.

INGREDIENTS OF BLACK POWDER
(EARLY GUNPOWDER)

POTASSIUM NITRATE

SULFUR

POWDERED CHARCOAL

guns, it made a lot of thick smoke. When it was used in battles, it was very hard for soldiers to see on the battlefield through all the smoke. The commanding officers couldn't see what was happening and therefore did not have the information they needed to give good orders. Gunpowder also wasn't powerful enough to propel bullets toward targets that were far away. A less smoky, more powerful explosive was needed for battle.

Two inventions revolutionized the field of explosives. The first was the invention of guncotton by Professor C. F. Schönbein in Basle, Switzerland, in about 1845. He made it by treating cotton with nitric acid. It was much more explosive and less smoky than gunpowder, but for twenty years, no one knew how to handle it safely. Sir Frederick Abel figured out how to make it safe, but not until late in the 1860s. In 1846, Professor Ascanio Sobrero discovered nitroglycerin in Turin, Italy. This oil was made by pouring glycerin into a mixture of nitric acid and sulfuric acid. It was incredibly explosive and not very smoky, but very hard to handle. No one knew how to detonate, or set off, the oil reliably and safely.

Both of these inventions were dangerous. People were killed in accidents making and transporting the materials. Gunpowder's replacement needed to be powerful and smokeless, but also safe to make, ship, use, and easy to light. By the early 1860s, guncotton and nitroglycerin were interesting ideas, but couldn't do these things.

THE NOBELS AND NITROGLYCERIN

In the early 1860s, Alfred and Immanuel Nobel became very interested in explosives, particularly in how nitroglycerin might be used. Sometime during 1854 or 1855, one of the Nobels' tutors had shown them the explosive power of nitroglycerin. As Alfred Nobel later wrote, "The first time I saw nitro-glycerine was in the beginning of the Crimean War. Professor Sinin in St. Petersburg exhibited some to my father and me, and struck on an anvil to show that only the part touched by the hammer exploded without spreading. His opinion was that it might become a useful substance for military purposes, if only a practical means could be devised to explode it." This experiment fascinated Alfred Nobel. The nitroglycerin wouldn't always explode if it was lit with a normal fuse. Sometimes nitroglycerin just burned brightly without exploding. How could this powerful explosive be harnessed?

Alfred Nobel started experimenting with nitroglycerin in St. Petersburg. Immanuel and Alfred both tried mixing nitroglycerin with gunpowder, but couldn't make it explode reliably. However, mixing the two made the new material easier to handle. By 1862, Alfred had started setting the mixture alight with a fuse. He made the mixture explode on top of the ice on the Neva Canal in St. Petersburg as Robert and Ludvig watched.

Immanuel then wrote to Alfred saying that he knew how to make the new explosive work well. The Russians were interested in using it and offered Immanuel money to show them how well it worked. Alfred went to Stockholm to see Immanuel and talk about the experiments. When he returned to St. Petersburg, he wrote a long letter to his father.

When you first wrote to me in Petersburg, you gave me to understand that the new explosive powder was a fully developed invention, and that it was twenty times as powerful as ordinary gunpowder. . . . At your request, I came to Sweden, where I found that your figures were built on an inconclusive experiment using a lead pipe. The result of my visit was a complete fiasco and proved that by then you had given up altogether the idea of the glycerine powder, considering it impractical or not sufficiently developed.

Alfred was embarrassed by Immanuel's claims to the Russians because Immanuel had nothing like this incredible explosive to show them. It seems that Alfred felt his father had wasted his time and effort when he was doing such interesting work himself.

Alfred Nobel called the nitroglycerin "blasting oil" because he thought people would find the name easier to remember. This was the beginning of Nobel's serious career as an inventor and businessman. He later wrote, "Although my father had first hit on mixing nitroglycerine with gunpowder, he considered, on account of his unsuccess, the invention as mine and desired me to patent it in my name, which I did." Alfred Nobel applied for his first patent for "manufacturing powder both for blasting and shooting purposes." The description can be confusing, because the words "powder" and "oil" are often used in talking about blasting oil. It was, in fact, still an oil, even though for some time the gunpowder was mixed in with it. Later, the nitroglycerin was used on its own. The patent for producing blasting oil was granted to him in Sweden, France, England, and Belgium before he turned thirty in 1863. Soon he would become famous. At the beginning of 1863 he moved back to Sweden to live with his parents at Heleneborg in Stockholm.

Af de olika sätten att i enlighet med Nobels patenterade uppfinning, d. v. s. *medelst krúts eller liknande ämnens
explosion, åstadkomma en detonations-impuls eller stöt, som är
nödrändig för att bringa nitroglycerinen i explosion,* äro föl-
jande de lämpligaste

Nödiga redskap:

1) Ett graderadt mått rymmande 1 ℔ sprängolja, hvarpå
   hvarje 10 ort kunna afläsas.
2) Ett långt rör, hvarigenom oljan hälles i borrhålet.
3) Patenterade knallhattar.
4) Tändproppar.
5) Stubintråd.
6) Patroner med dertill hörande tändproppar för horison-
   tala eller lighål samt för otäta borrhål.

Om laddningen.

1. Med knallhatt och vattenförladdning.

Sprängoljan hälles i borrhålet genom det ofvan nämnda
röret.

Borrhålet fylles sedermera
med vatten

Knallhatten påträdes ena än-
dan af stubintråden och tätgöres
med beck, vax eller dylikt, hvar-
efter den nedsänkes tätt under
ytan af sprängoljan.

Förklaring af teckningen.

a Berget.
b Borrhålet.
c Sprängoljans yta.
d Vattnets yta.
e Stubinen.
f Knallhatten.
Obs. Sandförladdning kan äfven
brukas; i detta fall förses stubintråden
med en bricka af träd eller kork för att
hindra sandens nedrasande i sprängoljan.

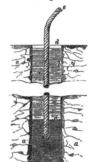

Patents must include very clear and explicit descriptions of the materials and process used to make the thing patented. This is a clearly labeled page from one of Alfred Nobel's patents for nitroglycerin in Sweden.

Patents

A patent is basically an agreement between the person who invents something and the country in which he or she wants to make or sell it. The inventor describes the secret of how it is made, and the country grants the inventor all the rights to money made from the invention. The invention needs to be a new idea or a change to an existing idea that makes it more useful. Every country has its own patent laws, and an inventor has to apply for a patent in each one. A patent doesn't last forever. In the United States today, a patent only lasts for twenty years.

THE BLASTING CAP AND DYNAMITE

Nobel needed to show industrial decision makers how well his blasting oil worked. He asked a local mining company near Stockholm to let him test it in their mines. He wrote this letter after the tests.

Stockholm, 2nd January, 1864
Herrn Otto Schwartzmann
General Manager of the Ammeberg Works

Dear Sir,

While you were abroad, Herr Beck was kind enough to allow me to carry out experiments in your mines, with a powder for which I hold patents both here and abroad.

These provisional experiments seem to have proved the superior quality of the powder in question. As it is more powerful . . . the amount of the charge can be lessened or greater quantities of rock can be blasted.

Its main advantage is, I believe, in the saving of labor.

After these tests, orders started coming in for blasting oil. Newspapers and magazines in Sweden, Germany, England, Belgium, and France wrote about it and asked Alfred Nobel questions about it. Immanuel and Alfred founded a nitroglycerin factory in Heleneborg next to their house. It was a very small operation with only four other employees, including Alfred's younger brother Emil. They made blasting oil for companies such as the Ammeberg Works and Northern Railways.

Alfred Nobel concentrated mostly on experiments. He never worked well as part of a team, and he didn't get much inspiration from bouncing around ideas with other people. He usually worked alone, often for eighteen hours at a stretch. He would go on marathons of experimentation without paying attention to his health. Then he would need a complete rest when the spell was over. Emil and Immanuel were also active experimenters. It seems Immanuel might have had an argument with Alfred. He stayed away from the Heleneborg lab, working on experiments with torpedoes instead. The Nobel men were all known for

The Nobels set up a factory by their house at Heleneborg.

their clever, questioning minds and were always looking for better ways to do things.

Alfred Nobel had performed many experiments with the nitroglycerin and gunpowder mix in St. Petersburg. He wrote to his father before he moved back to Sweden, "I . . . actually succeeded in bringing about an astonishing effect underwater on a small scale. This was done . . . by using glass pipes surrounded by powder." What he had done was surround the blasting oil with pure gunpowder, and set the gunpowder alight using a normal fuse made of braided fibers that was a bit like string. This created a powerful explosion, but only underwater. It made him think about how best to detonate the blasting oil.

At the laboratory in Heleneborg Alfred Nobel spent many long days and nights experimenting. He knew that the fuse and gunpowder method alone would not reliably make a large enough amount of blasting oil explode. Nitroglycerin explodes when hit by a hammer because of the heat created by the shock waves made by the impact of the hammer on the oil. Nobel was trying to create something that would send shock waves through a whole mass of blasting oil and make it explode on cue. It took him about fifty experiments to come up with the solution. He needed to make a large enough initial explosion to force the bigger nitroglycerin explosion to occur.

THE BREAKTHROUGH

Nobel filled a wooden plug with gunpowder and then put a fuse in it and packed blasting oil below it. When the fuse was lit, the gunpowder exploded, and the shock wave was forced down through the blasting oil, making it explode. The plug stopped the shock wave from traveling out the top instead of going through the oil, rather like the water had done when Nobel exploded the glass tubes underwater. Nobel called this invention the initial igniter, but it later became known as the blasting cap. This was a huge breakthrough in explosive technology. It was used to detonate explosives for more than sixty years. No one had managed to unleash nitroglycerin's explosive potential before. Suddenly, the

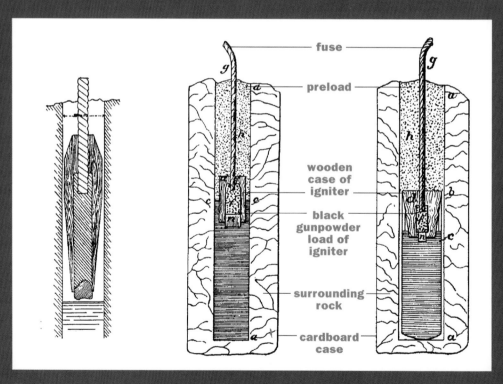

The blasting cap changed over time as Nobel improved it. The first version is on the left. On the right is a cross section of a later design.

breakthrough that industry needed was made. Nobel was granted a patent for the blasting cap early in 1864. Many people think this was his most important invention and the one that shaped the world the most.

As he kept working on his invention, Nobel made it better. He started using a very small amount of another explosive called fulminate of mercury instead of the gunpowder. He also exchanged the wooden plug for a copper capsule. This smaller and more explosive blasting cap was even better and easier to manufacture.

Robert Nobel visited Heleneborg in September 1863. He wrote a letter to Alfred the following May.

> My Good Alfred,
>
> Give up inventing as soon as possible. It only brings disappointment. You have such wide knowledge and such exceptional qualities that you should turn your attention to more serious matters. If I had your knowledge and your capacities I would spread my wings, even in this wretched country of Finland . . .

Thankfully, Alfred did not give up inventing because by that point, he had already made nitroglycerin useable and invented the blasting cap. Alfred Nobel himself wrote as part of a patent application in 1864, "I am the first to have brought these subjects from the area of Science to that of Industry." Nobel expected his discoveries to earn him and his family money and fame because of their practical applications in the world of industry.

After the explosion at Heleneborg, there was nothing left of the factory. At the time, there were few chances for such large explosions to happen, since explosives technology was so new. Today we can create much bigger explosions easily, but at the time only natural disasters such as earthquakes could wreak this kind of destruction.

FOUR

Nitroglycerin Panic

In 1864, solving the problem of storing and handling nitroglycerin safely suddenly became very important to Alfred Nobel. By September 1864, there was a great deal—about 250 pounds (113 kilograms)—of blasting oil stored at Heleneborg for a big railway order. No one thought it was particularly dangerous. On September 3, Alfred's brother Emil and one other worker were making new oil in the factory. Without any warning, the laboratory and the rest of the factory blew up. Emil and four other people were killed. Tragically, Emil was only twenty years old and becoming a good scientist in his own right. No one knows exactly what caused the explosion. The family was horrified, as were their neighbors. The local newspaper wrote:

In the capital [Stockholm] people heard the violent sound of the explosion and saw a huge, yellow flame rise straight up into the air. It was replaced within moments by an enormous pillar of smoke that also disappeared so quickly. . . . There was nothing left of the factory . . . except a few charred fragments thrown here and there. . . . Most ghastly was the sight of the mutilated corpses strewn on the ground. . . . The effect of the explosion could be judged by the fact that in a nearby stone house, the walls facing the factory had split open, and a woman who had been standing by the stove cooking had part of her head crushed, one arm torn off, and one thigh terribly mauled. [She lived.]

Alfred Nobel was hurt by glass and wood that hit his head, but he recovered quickly. He started work again the day after the disaster. Both Alfred and Immanuel immediately threw themselves into the problem of keeping their business going. People were suddenly very aware of nitroglycerin and very scared of it. Immanuel wrote a paper describing how he thought the accident had happened, because Emil might have been making nitroglycerin through a process that was different from the usual method. The different process may have made the

Emil Nobel was very young when he died. This photo was taken soon before the explosion at Heleneborg.

materials particularly explosive and unstable. The batch Emil was working on may have exploded, and the shock wave from that explosion may have blown up the rest of the stock stored there. Immanuel tried to make people feel safer by stating how the oil should be made and why it might have been so dangerous on September 3. He said, "An accident of this nature should not occur again during nitroglycerin manufacture."

Alfred never wrote or spoke about how he felt about the explosion. He must have been very upset about his brother's death because it is known that they were good friends. Perhaps he was too upset to let anyone know how badly he felt. On October 6, 1864, the Nobel family experienced another tragedy when Immanuel suffered a major stroke. He never recovered and could never walk or stand again. It is speculated that the stroke happened because of the stress of the disaster and the real chance that his family would lose everything again.

Alfred Nobel put his energy into trying to find a place to manufacture blasting oil. Because most of Stockholm was frightened of it, this was a difficult task. The government banned explosives factories within the city. After only a month, Nobel hit on a solution. He set up a factory on a barge moored in Lake Mälaren in Bockholmssund, near Stockholm. It was only 10 miles (16 kilometers) from Stockholm, but it was outside the reach of the city government. He had to move the barge a few times because some of the people who lived on the shore were angry about its presence. Then the Swedish government placed a large order for blasting oil only five weeks after the accident. It needed to build an important tunnel for the state railway line.

After the disaster, money became a problem. Alfred Nobel was afraid that people would make claims for compensation, or money to

For a short time after the explosion at Heleneborg, the Nobels manufactured nitroglycerin on this barge, moored in Lake Mälaren.

pay for their ruined property or lost business. He worked quickly to reorganize the way his business was set up. New partners were included who provided cash and status to the business. The main partner was Johann Wilhelm Smitt, who had made a fortune in South America. In November 1864, Alfred, Immanuel, Smitt, and Carl Wennerström set up a company called Nitroglycerin Aktiebolaget.

A BETTER YEAR

On January 21, 1865, the Nobels moved production off the barge and into a new explosives factory near Stockholm. The place was called Vinterviken. This factory kept making explosives for fifty years, but it had a slow start. By the end of February it had made only 100 pounds (45 kg) of blasting oil, but by August it was going strong with more than 2 tons made. People around the world were still aware of how dangerous blasting oil was, but they also needed it to keep building roads, railways, and towns for their growing populations. Alfred Nobel hired his childhood friend Alarik Liedbeck to work with him in Vinterviken. They had met in school before the Nobels moved to Russia, but had lost touch over the years. When Nobel needed an engineer to help run the factory, he offered Liedbeck the job because he was an excellent engineer who had Nobel's trust. They worked together for the rest of their lives, making new machinery and ways to produce explosives.

Business grew so quickly that the Vinterviken factory was soon overwhelmed. The company needed to expand. Alfred Nobel decided it was time to open factories outside of Sweden. As well as having workers available, Germany was a good choice because many orders came from German companies, and Germany had good trade relationships with many other countries. Nobel started a company called Alfred Nobel & Co. Then he moved to Hamburg, Germany, and built a factory nearby in Krümmel. It opened on June 20, 1865. Nobel also sold the right to make nitroglycerin in Norway to someone else, who paid enough for him to send his parents to a spa for a rest. The next big market to expand into was the United States.

In 1865, the nitroglycerin factory in Krümmel looked like this.

Alfred Nobel was busy running his companies, doing everything from the handling of the finances to the engineering to the sales. Doing business was very different then. The mail was slow, the telephone did not exist yet, and there were no faxes or e-mail. There wasn't even airmail because there were no airplanes yet. People had to meet face to face or write letters in order to conduct business. Newspapers and magazines helped pass around information. Nobel wrote many letters to newspapers and to other inventors, sharing information and helping correct erroneous information. He was always traveling, meeting important clients, and selling the idea of blasting oil. He also kept working on his blasting caps and finally found a way to produce them and sell them.

Alfred Nobel knew that the demand for blasting oil in the United States was huge. The country was going through a period of rapid growth. People building railways, harbors, mines, and buildings all needed explosives to keep this pace going. Gunpowder was still the most widely used explosive. A U.S. company called Du Pont de Nemours made gunpowder locally. Although Nobel had applied for a U.S. patent on blasting oil, he had problems getting it. Nobel knew that a nitroglycerin factory was needed in the United States. Nobel sailed for New York at the end of March 1866.

MORE DISASTERS

No one ever really found out why the factory at Heleneborg blew up. Besides this one big disaster, there had been few accidents in making, transporting, or using blasting oil. Alfred Nobel wrote later that, "liquid nitroglycerin had not yet proved unmanageable."

Some of the stories told about how blasting oil was moved around and carelessly handled are very frightening to think about now. To people not used to the properties of explosive oil, it looked like milk. Many people didn't pay attention to how dangerous the oil was, and how easily it could explode. The factory at Krümmel shipped blasting oil in metal cans, which were laid in sawdust inside wooden crates. Often the cans would leak, and blasting oil would run out of the crates. This meant that blasting oil collected in ships' cargo holds and on trucks' wheels. Leaked oil was used to grease wheels and oil harnesses and boots. In Wales, cans of blasting oil were used as soccer balls until one man was blown up. Alfred Nobel himself helped dig frozen nitroglycerin out of a tank using a kind of axe, even though he should have known better. He also traveled with bottles of nitroglycerin in his luggage.

Shipping Problems

Getting nitroglycerin to the East Coast of the United States was fairly easy because it could leave Germany and sail straight to a port such as New York. However, most of the demand was in the Midwest and on the West Coast where people were settling in great numbers. This meant that ships either had to go all the way to the bottom of South America and around Cape Horn, then back up the Pacific coast, or they had to stop on the Atlantic coast of Panama. Because the Panama Canal didn't exist yet, the oil had to be sent by wagon over jungle roads and then put back on different ships to go up the Pacific coast.

In the spring of 1866, this lack of respect for the explosive came to an end. A string of disasters around the world started another nitroglycerin panic, much like the smaller one in Stockholm that occurred after the Heleneborg disaster. A crate of nitroglycerin blew up after being stored behind the desk at a New York hotel, injuring nineteen people. On March 4, a large explosion in Sydney, Australia, destroyed a warehouse in which two cases of nitroglycerin had been stored. Several nearby houses collapsed. Then, on April 3, the steamship *European* blew up, killing forty-seven people. It was off Aspinwall on the Atlantic coast of Panama when the cargo of nitroglycerin exploded. A German ship called *Mosel* that was full of nitroglycerin blew up before it left port, killing eighty-four people. Later in April, the Wells, Fargo & Co. warehouse in San Francisco exploded, killing fifteen people. It had been storing nitroglycerin.

Nobel's partner in San Francisco, Julius Bandmann, also was puzzled by some of the problems with nitroglycerin. He wrote Nobel this letter on April 30, 1866.

In view of this second terrible disaster which has occurred at Aspinwall . . . we must, no doubt, give up any hope of finding a ready market for it [nitroglycerin] at an early date. . . . In our last letter we called your attention to the sulphuric acid smell and the hissing of the two cases that were opened in the warehouses of the Pacific Railroad, and we shall be glad to hear from you about this. To-day we have to add that we put the first case of oil into champagne bottles, and stored these in the house where the other cases were.

We have been compelled to take them away from there, and have not been able to find any place for them yet. . . . Herr Nielsen and some Chinamen have put the chests into a small boat, and have anchored her with some of the champagne bottles about five miles from the town. What can this mean, unless it is that the oil is beginning to decompose. If this process of decomposition continues unchecked, would it not be possible for spontaneous combustion to ensue, although some time may elapse before the oil becomes dangerous. When would such danger occur, or would it never occur? Why was it that the first case, on being opened, gave off practically no odour at all, while the other two cases had a coppery smell, and why did the oil make a sizzling noise when the cork was drawn? These are important questions for us, and we should be glad if you would answer them. . . .

The 'Central Pacific Railroad' alone consumes about 300 kegs of gunpowder [each keg about 25 pounds {11 kg} of gunpowder] a day. It is therefore worth while to introduce your oil.

IN NEW YORK

Nobel faced a lot of negative public opinion when he arrived in New York. He tried to tell people how useful and relatively safe he thought blasting oil was by writing letters to newspapers. He met with the mayor of New York City. He gave demonstrations of how to handle nitroglycerin, showing that it just burned when set alight and didn't explode when dropped. He offered the opinion that the accidents must have occurred when packing material such as sawdust near the nitroglycerin got soaked with it and was then set on fire, raising the temperature around the oil high enough to make it explode.

People were still afraid. Some states passed laws that said any deaths caused by transporting blasting oil would be considered to be murders. Congress was thinking about laws to pass about blasting oil. General Henry Du Pont was head of Du Pont de Nemours, the U.S. gunpowder manufacturing company. His opinion was often quoted. "It's just a question of time how soon a man who uses nitroglycerin will pay with his life." While Nobel was in the United States in May, the Nobel factory in Krümmel blew up. News traveled so slowly that it took two weeks for Nobel to hear of it. The Norwegian factory also exploded a few weeks later.

While in the United States, Nobel wanted to perform some experiments to see if he could make nitroglycerin safer to transport. He found a way to add methyl alcohol to nitroglycerin. This made it less sensitive

Du Pont de Nemours made gunpowder in the United States. Nitroglycerin challenged gunpowder's hold on the U.S. explosives market. But even Du Pont had to change with the times, and later it made dynamite.

and safer to transport. He set up a series of companies with U.S. partners Taliafero Shaffner and Otto Bürstenbinder. Shaffner earlier had claimed that he should have the U.S. patent for blasting oil. These partners were not trustworthy, however, and the companies had problems. Nobel had to make decisions quickly, so he could not always do the wisest thing.

Nobel finally set up a company without Shaffner and Bürstenbinder called the Atlantic Giant Powder Company. Congress agreed to allow blasting oil to be manufactured and shipped around the United States, but regulated how it had to be packaged so it was safe. Nobel arrived back in Germany on August 10. On August 14, 1866, he was granted the U.S. patent for blasting oil.

Sometimes disasters can help people learn new things. In this case, industrial leaders saw how well blasting oil worked because of the series of tragic explosions. They started ordering great amounts of blasting oil. They wanted to put it to good use in their projects.

Thomas Edison and Nitroglycerin

Thomas Edison was a young man working in Boston when he read about Alfred Nobel's explosives. He and a friend decided to make some nitroglycerin for themselves in 1868. Edison wrote in his diary, "To see if the quality was O.K. we exploded a few drops and the results were so strong that we both got frightened, so we put the nitro in a pop bottle, . . . tied a cord to the end of the bottle and let it down a sewer."

When he got back to Germany, Nobel had to work hard to get the factory at Krümmel going again. By this time, Sweden was having problems. Farmers' crops had failed, so people didn't have enough food or work in the countryside. This led to financial difficulty for people in most industries. Many Swedes left their homes and moved to places where they could get work and feed their families. A great number of them went to work in Krümmel. Skilled workers from Vinterviken went to Krümmel, too, to teach the newcomers what to do. The factory was soon working again, and many orders were coming in. Nobel's factories in New York and San Francisco grew to meet the demand in the United States as well.

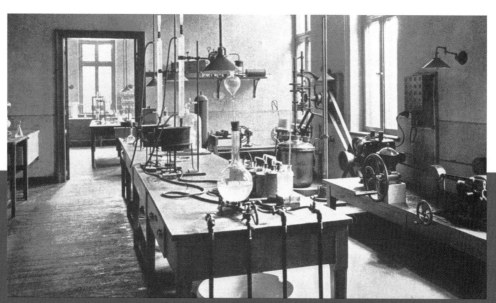

Although lab equipment has improved a great deal since the 1860s, you may still recognize some of the equipment from this lab at Krümmel. Nobel and many of the engineers and scientists working at Krümmel used the labs to solve problems and develop new processes on a daily basis.

FIVE

Dynamite

By 1866, most of the world knew about blasting oil. Some people were afraid of its power, while others were interested in using that power. When used with a blasting cap, blasting oil was reliable. Now that Nobel knew how dangerous it truly was, he wanted to make an explosive that he was sure was safe to transport and use.

An experiment in Krümmel led to the invention of dynamite in 1866. Nobel developed the name "dynamite" from the Greek word *dynamis*, which means power. This invention would make Alfred Nobel's name known worldwide. He had been toying with the invention for a few years. He took the nitroglycerin oil and added silica, which absorbed the oil. Silica is like white sand. It made a kind of paste that could be shaped and handled far more easily than nitroglycerin could on its own. There were three main advantages to the paste. First, it didn't freeze as easily as nitroglycerin. Nitroglycerin on its own froze at a relatively high temperature, and defrosting it for use was very dangerous. Second, the paste was easier to ship and transport than nitroglycerin because it didn't tend to blow up without warning like nitroglycerin sometimes did. Third, it could be shaped into cylinders and placed exactly where it was needed. Sometimes, nitroglycerin oil would seep further into rock than the engineers wanted it to and could explode later, when no one expected it to.

Nobel tried mixing many materials with nitroglycerin before finding the perfect one, kieselguhr. Kieselguhr is a type of rock made up of shells and tiny aquatic plants. There was plenty of this material along the banks of the Elbe River in Germany. It is so absorbent that a mixture of one-quarter kieselguhr and three-quarters nitroglycerin becomes a solid instead of a liquid. This new material was molded into cylinders. It wouldn't explode unless a fuse was put into it. It was much easier to ship and use, but only a quarter less explosive than blasting oil alone.

Nobel explained in June 1874 why he had wanted to replace nitroglycerin with dynamite.

Dynamite Today

Dynamite's chemical makeup has changed a little, but it is still widely used today. Most of its explosive force is used by companies to blast mines and quarries. Tunnels are made using dynamite. A great deal of underwater blasting is done with dynamite. Some military explosives still use dynamite too.

. . . if nitro-glycerine had continued to be used as an explosive substance we should have found means to make it perfectly safe in handling by not using metallic packing, and using some other precautions, but it was more easy to convey it into a solid. My objection to nitro-glycerine was less from the difficulty of carrying it than from its liquid state, which causes it to leak into the crevices of bore-holes, thus getting filtered into the rock, and causing accidents, difficult to prevent, that was my chief reason for going over to dynamite. . . . whilst nitro-glycerine with a small sale gave rise to many accidents, dynamite in spite of a large trade has caused none.

Some countries were very worried about nitroglycerin and the accidents that it caused. They passed laws that limited how it could be made or transported. Nobel had to make sure his companies followed these laws. As dynamite replaced nitroglycerin, most of the laws got easier to follow or were changed because dynamite was so much safer.

This horse drawn carriage is full of a load of dynamite. Dynamite is much easier and safer to transport than nitroglycerin.

BUSINESS CONCERNS

By this time, Nobel had a growing number of patents in many different countries. Because patents are very specific, each new invention needed a new patent. Each country Nobel wanted to sell his invention in required him to apply for a different patent too. After some early mistakes, Nobel always wrote his own patent applications. Blasting oil, dynamite, and blasting caps were all patented in many European countries and in the United States. Sometimes, dishonest companies would use Nobel's patented ways of making items to make their own and not pay him a royalty, or part of the profit. Asking for patents and defending his rights to patents that had been granted took Nobel a great deal of time.

Nobel also needed to keep expanding his companies to keep up with the demand for his explosives. Nobel spent a lot of time traveling between his factories. He always stayed in charge of his whole business empire, but he needed reliable people in his companies to run the day-to-day operations. As the businesses grew, he had hundreds of people making important decisions. Some of the people he trusted betrayed him, stole his money, or tried to pass off his ideas as their own. However, many were loyal and helpful, such as his good friend Alarik Liedbeck.

When a new invention is put into production, new ways of making it have to be developed. At Heleneborg back in 1863, all the blasting oil was made by hand in small batches. By 1867, Nobel's companies made 11 tons of dynamite, too much to make by hand. Engineers and scientists in Nobel's businesses had to think up new machines and processes to help produce dynamite and blasting caps more quickly, easily, and safely. Nobel liked to hire ex-soldiers as workers because he thought they were very disciplined and good at following orders. He felt this helped keep people safe during the dangerous process of making and shipping explosives.

FAMILY TIES

Nobel was then a successful inventor and businessman in his thirties. He had plenty of money coming in and a bright future because it seemed his explosives would always be in demand. He never stopped inventing and enlarging his businesses. Despite his incredible productivity, Nobel was often ill. He never took a break to rest himself fully. He would stop

Dynamite Destruction

Not all of Nobel's explosives were put to good use. Because dynamite was cheap and fairly easy to get, it became a weapon used by terrorists. People who were unhappy with the way their governments ruled could use dynamite to try to injure the people in charge. It was set under thrones, on bridges to be exploded as people passed over them, and thrown through windows. From 1872 on, terrorists from Russia to Chicago relied on it.

to recover when his health got worse, but then push forward as soon as he was well enough, but not entirely well. He said that he disliked all the frantic activity his businesses demanded and felt burdened by his worries. He liked to spend time alone, working or thinking.

Nobel never married. Some of his writings seem to imply that he was afraid having a wife and children would stop him from working so much. He didn't want to lose control of the empire he was building. He did see this as a sacrifice. Nobel wrote that he lived a kind of half-life, and that he was not a whole person, because he didn't have those kinds of family ties.

He did, however, have strong ties with his brothers. For their whole lives, the three brothers kept working together, even when they were geographically far apart. Robert worked with Alfred in the explosives business and moved back to Russia in 1870 to work with Ludvig. Ludvig and Robert grew to be the most powerful petroleum oil dealers in Russia. Ludvig went on to become so famous that he is better known

Ludvig Nobel, Alfred's brother, was a friend and business partner most of his life.

in Russia than Alfred even today. Alfred was also involved with their business. Ludvig's first wife died in 1869, but he remarried in 1870. Alfred cared about his brothers' families and children, staying in touch with their activities and sending advice.

Immanuel and Andriette stayed in Sweden. Alfred visited his parents and helped them out as much as he could. Immanuel kept inventing after his stroke. His body was weak, but his mind was very active. Andriette looked after him and took him on trips to spas to allow him to try and get his strength back. In 1868, Alfred and Immanuel were jointly given the Letterstedt Prize for "important discoveries of practical value to humanity." The prize was given by the Royal Swedish Academy of Sciences, and Immanuel kept the medal they received.

Despite his problems in Sweden, Immanuel wanted to help his homeland. He wrote three illustrated books, one on land mines called *Cheap Defense of the Country's Roads*, one on sea mines called *Cheap Defense of Archipelagos*, and one called *Proposal for the Country's Defense: A New Year's Gift to the Swedish People, 1871*. Immanuel also came up with the idea for plywood, which was laughed at when he published it in 1870. Now plywood is one of the main materials used in house and furniture construction around the world. When he died in 1872, Immanuel was still developing his ideas.

Immanuel's last letter to Alfred was sent on December 26, 1871. He wrote, "A hearty hug is sent to you, the last one this year, from your old parents, who take great gladness in having such sons who only give us joy and never sorrow." Alfred may never have had his own children, but he always had a loving family who supported him and understood his work.

Alfred Nobel moved into this mansion in the heart of fashionable Paris in 1873.

Paris and New Ideas

In 1873 Alfred Nobel was forty years old. His businesses were growing quickly, and he was busy experimenting and inventing. However, he was often ill. He had rheumatism, a disease that made his joints ache, so he walked slightly bent over. He was still a Swedish citizen and went back to the country as often as he could to visit his mother and cousins. However, he wrote, "My country is wherever I work, and I work everywhere."

Nobel wanted to be closer to Europe's economic center. Paris was the center of European business at the time, so Nobel decided to leave Hamburg and move there. He bought a mansion in Paris. As his businesses became more established, Nobel stopped traveling as often as he had. He settled more into life in Paris. He enjoyed living in Paris, which he thought was a fine, civilized city.

Nobel's house was impressively large and had a good laboratory. There was a greenhouse on the side of the house where he could grow orchids all year. He had opera music to play. He also hung paintings by Swedish and French artists and changed them every few weeks. The furniture and decoration of the mansion were heavy and impressive as was the fashion at the time.

Nobel had handsome horses sent over from Russia to pull his carriage so he could go travel the city fashionably. The mansion was near a park called the Bois de Boulogne, where he could go for carriage rides or pleasant walks. Nobel sometimes went for walks, both in the park and along the sidewalks, where cafés and shops were filled with people enjoying life.

Nobel followed the current fashion in his dress and his home. Like most men at the time, Nobel wore a beard. He always dressed in a dark

Paris in the Late 1800s

In the 1850s, Paris had an epidemic of cholera, which is a disease spread by dirty food or drinking water. To stop the epidemic, the city was rebuilt with new sewers, water supplies, roads, and buildings. Napoleon III's empire collapsed in 1870 during the war between France and Prussia. The city fell into chaos. In 1871, the French lost the war and a socialist government called the Paris Commune took over briefly. Prussian troops occupied the city until 1873. In 1875, a republic was formed with an elected president. Soon, the political storm subsided and art, science, and intellectual work bloomed.

suit, white shirt, and tie. Even though Nobel wrote that he didn't care what people thought of him, he clearly thought it was important to fit in with the fashions of the time. Maybe he just didn't want to stand out or be thought of as unusual.

Sometimes, Nobel gave banquets. He invited guests to stay in his mansion. Some were business contacts; some were family members visiting from Sweden and Russia. Sometimes, his home was full of family, and other times it was used as a business conference center in which he held important meetings.

It looks like Nobel had every chance to enjoy his life, and perhaps he did. It's hard to know for certain because his letters were filled mostly with complaints about his health or how he never got any rest. At home, Nobel began the day by opening and answering his mail. He got hundreds

This shows what fashionable men in Paris wore in the late 1800s. The buildings were usually decorated in an ornate, elaborate way, as this illustration shows.

of letters inviting him to parties and dinners, asking about business deals, discussing inventions and experiments, and asking for money. Nobel was asked for about $4,000 every day, which was a very large sum of money at the time. Nobel also read the important newspapers from France, England, and Germany.

Nobel often performed experiments in his laboratory. He hired an assistant, Georges Fehrenbach, to work with him there. Nobel worked long days, often twelve to fourteen hours. The nitroglycerin he experimented with gave him headaches. He was regularly found lying down on the laboratory floor recovering, or working with his head wrapped in cold bandages.

Nobel had started working with Paul Barbe, his French partner, in 1868. Nobel described Barbe in a letter to Robert in 1883: "He has a marvelous scientific imagination, is an exceptionally good salesman, a far-seeing business man, and knows how to make the best of people . . . but he is unreliable unless his personal interest is involved." Together Nobel and Barbe reorganized the

Paul Barbe worked closely with Nobel until his death.

way most of Nobel's companies were set up. In 1875 they created a scientific advisory board for their dynamite factories. Alarik Liedbeck from Vinterviken was put in charge of it.

THE NEXT GREAT IDEA

The story of how Nobel created his next great invention shows the strange way ideas can be born. For a while, Nobel had been working to improve dynamite. It was a safe and useful explosive, but it wasn't perfect. When it got very wet or was pressed hard, it tended to sweat drops of nitroglycerin. Because it had only three-quarters of the power of pure nitroglycerin, dynamite didn't work on very strong rock. Nobel was looking for a material that would contain nitroglycerin in a solid form, but also keep its strength as an explosive. He tried getting guncotton, an explosive in fabric form, to absorb nitroglycerin, but it didn't work.

One day in 1875, Nobel cut his finger. At the time, people didn't have adhesive bandages. Nobel used something called collodion on his cut. Collodion is sticky and is made when guncotton is dissolved in another chemical called ether. The pain in his finger kept Nobel awake, so he went back into his laboratory to work. It was four o'clock in the morning. Nobel started thinking about using the same kind of chemical process that made collodion to make a guncotton and nitroglycerin mix. By nine o'clock when Fehrenbach came to work, Nobel had successfully done it. He gave the first demonstration of his new invention, called gelignite or blasting gelatin.

Blasting gelatin was more explosive than even plain nitroglycerin, but it was safe to transport. Water didn't alter it, so it could even be used

Rainmaker

Dynamite had some odd uses. One of the strangest but most helpful was for making rain. Long periods without rain could ruin farmers and also make cities unhealthy places in which to live. In the 1880s, people actually made it rain in New York City by detonating 200 pounds (90.7 kg) of dynamite sent up by balloon over the city. In Texas, dynamite sent into the sky caused thunder and rain.

underwater. Depending on how much guncotton was mixed with nitroglycerin, it could be made more or less explosive. The most explosive kind was high in guncotton and looked like jelly. Less explosive blasting gelatin was wobblier and looked more like yogurt or custard.

Once again, Nobel had made industrial explosives even better. Using the new blasting gelatin instead of dynamite saved money, time, and work. Within a year most of Nobel's dynamite factories switched to making blasting gelatin. In Great Britain, the government took longer to be convinced of blasting gelatin's safety. It took until 1884, when Sir Frederick Abel said that it was "in every respect the most perfect explosive known."

SEVEN

A Lonely Man

Nobel wrote a letter in 1878, saying, "Only a few years ago, I longed for the big city with its hectic life. Today I long to go away from here to enjoy a period of earthly calm in a serene place to prepare for the everlasting peace." He was often depressed, driven to keep working and experimenting, but kept down by his continuing bad health. Nobel complained about being unhappy and feeling lonely, but he also turned down invitations to parties and events at which he could meet people. He worried that people were only interested in him for his money, or because he was the dynamite king.

Nobel seemed to enjoy exchanging scientific ideas and talking about literature and arts. He also seemed to have to force himself to go to places where he could do these things. Even though Nobel read the world news, he was more interested in philosophy, science, and literature.

He liked to think about how the world and people in it worked, how they thought, and how they learned. Despite being very busy with keeping his companies going and experimenting, he found time to read and discuss what he learned. He met Victor Hugo, the French writer, and they became friends. He met with other great thinkers, politicians, and artists at salons, which were small parties at which people met to talk about their ideas.

MEETING BERTHA

Nobel had a housekeeper and a valet to keep his house clean and his clothes and things in order. His food was plain and cooked to his liking. In 1876 he decided he needed a secretary to help him with his letters and records. He was in Vienna at the time, so he advertised in a Viennese newspaper. His advertisement said, "Wealthy, highly-educated elderly gentleman seeks lady of mature age, versed in languages, as secretary and supervisor of household."

One of the many women who replied to Nobel's advertisement was Countess Bertha Sofia Felitas Kinsky von Chinic und Tettau, known as Bertha Kinsky. Nobel liked the

When Bertha Kinsky met Alfred Nobel she was a young woman. Later in her life she became a crusader for peace.

clear and elegant letter she wrote. Although she had little money, she came from an upper-class family and knew how to treat important visitors. Kinsky was thirty-three years old, and had been working for the wealthy Suttner family in Vienna. She looked after the four daughters, teaching them music, languages, and manners. Then she and the Suttners' son fell in love. Bertha was poor and seven years older than Arthur was, so they were not allowed to marry. Kinsky had to leave her job and was very happy to hear from Nobel.

Nobel and Kinsky corresponded between Paris and Vienna. They agreed that Kinsky was to come work for him. Kinsky arrived in Paris at the beginning of May and was impressed by her new employer. She wrote,

> He made a very pleasant impression. In his advertisement he had described himself as an 'old gentlemen' and we had thought of him as a grey-haired invalid. But this was not the case; he was then only 43 years old, of somewhat less than average height, with a dark beard and features that were neither handsome nor ugly; his expression was a little gloomy, but this was softened by his kind blue eyes.

Nobel was redecorating a wing of his mansion for Kinsky, so she stayed in a hotel when she arrived. She and Nobel spent time together, conversing in four languages and driving through Paris. Kinsky and Nobel talked about explosives and war. Bertha wrote that Nobel wanted to make some machine or thing that would cause such "devastation that it would make wars altogether impossible." At the time, Kinsky had no extreme ideas about war, but she became a well-known pacifist later in her life. A pacifist is someone who believes in finding ways other than fighting and war to solve problems.

Kinsky and Nobel had a lot in common and enjoyed discussing their ideas about art, philosophy, and life in general. Nobel let her read the poem he had written about his childhood when he was eighteen years old. Perhaps Nobel was falling in love with Kinsky. He asked her if her heart was free. She told him about Arthur von Suttner, and he told her to wait for time to heal her wounds.

Kinsky missed Arthur von Suttner, and spent a lot of her time alone crying. After Kinsky had been in Paris for a week, Nobel had to travel for business. When he had been gone for two days von Suttner sent for Kinsky, and she went to Vienna to marry him in secret. For the next eleven years, Nobel and Kinsky wrote only a handful of letters to each other. However, she later helped Nobel decide how he was going to help the world become a more peaceful place.

ALFRED AND SOFIE

At the end of the summer of 1876, Nobel went to the town of Baden bei Wien near Vienna. Baden bei Wien was a resort town where people went to rest. Nobel met a twenty-year-old woman named Sofie Hess who was working in a flower shop. She bubbled with enthusiasm and flirted with Nobel. He fell in love with her and kept going back to Baden bei Wien whenever he could.

Nobel soon rented a house for Hess in Ischl, a resort in Austria. In 1880, he rented an apartment in Paris near his mansion for her to live in. A maid and a cook looked after her. She even had someone to teach her

French. Nobel sent Hess to fashionable spas and health resorts during the summer. She spent vast amounts of Nobel's money. She ran up bills and sometimes Nobel worried about how he would pay them. Nobel was never sure that he would not go bankrupt again someday.

When Nobel and Hess were in the same place, they met often, but they were usually apart. They wrote hundreds of letters to each other. Sometimes, they wrote every day. Hess wrote about money and everyday dramas. Nobel wrote about his business concerns, his health, and his opinions about other people. He valued Hess's openness about her emotions. Perhaps he felt that he could tell her about his emotions and his worries like he could with no one else.

Nobel wrote to Hess in May 1878, "It is one-thirty at night and the company executives have just left me, having tormented me all day with negotiations. . . . I have such a headache that I can hardly see to write." In August he wrote, "I am spending almost the whole day at home, working. Time passes slowly because I feel very lonely." Three days later he wrote, "[Alarik] Liedbeck arrived a few days ago. He sat beside me from morning to night, forcing me to holler until I go deaf myself. Today, for instance, he arrived at eight-thirty in the morning and not until a short while ago—at nine o'clock at night—could I get rid of him. Perhaps you can imagine how tired I am. Still I have to go on working . . ." A few days later he wrote, "I am absolutely convinced that my life is enormously more tedious than yours. My brother's relatives are pure torture. . . . I am finally rid of Liedbeck. . . . The man, whose heart is so fine and good, cannot grasp that his deafness is a great bother to others." Although he often complained in other letters, Nobel would never allow himself to be so honest with his other friends or family.

Nobel and Hess were linked together for nineteen years. He was first drawn to her uncomplicated, straightforward way of seeing the world. She clearly thought he was nice enough and liked how rich he was. Hess had very little education. Nobel valued an educated mind and thoughtful conversation more than almost anything else. He tried to teach her more things and show her more of how the world worked. Perhaps a different teacher could have changed Hess's manner and helped her learn a new way of thinking, but Nobel only grew more upset with her. She hated the way he wrote to her, as if he was better than she was.

Nobel never proposed marriage to her, but he started calling her Madame Nobel, which means Mrs. Nobel. Later, Nobel grew upset with Hess for using the last name Nobel, and asked her to stop. When Bertha von Suttner heard about Madame Nobel and wrote Nobel a card to congratulate him on his marriage, Nobel said he had neither a wife, nor a mistress.

EIGHT

International Success

Nobel's explosives businesses kept growing all around the world as demand for blasting gelatin mushroomed. Railways, mines, and roads kept being built and expanded. As these industries grew, the new oil industry began. It is hard to imagine it now, but no one knew how useful oil was until the 1850s. Before then, people lit their homes and workplaces with candles. Then, the kerosene lamp was invented. Suddenly, people could have brighter, more controllable light. Everyone wanted kerosene lamps, and there was a huge demand for kerosene to burn in them. Kerosene is made when oil is refined. Refining is the process that changes crude oil into useful materials.

Ludvig Nobel had become an important manufacturer in Russia. His company made military arms, such as rifles, as well as tools for industrial use. When Robert Nobel left Sweden to work with him in 1870, he was sent on a trip further into Russia to a place called Baku. He was looking for good trees to use for wooden rifle butts, but instead found crude oil in great amounts. Robert was excited about the chance of making money by selling the oil. Ludvig gave him the money he needed to set up a small company that drilled and refined oil. Ludvig wrote a letter to Alfred about Robert in 1875 that shows how strongly he felt about his ties to his brothers. "I always felt that we, that is you and I, ought to go down together [to Baku] and see if we cannot help him in any way. Since we have managed to achieve independence, we should try to help Robert to it, too."

Ludvig went to Baku without Alfred and was very happy with the progress of Robert's company. In 1877, Ludvig went to Paris to talk with

In the late 1800s people relied upon oil lamps to light their work and play. This family is using the light from an oil lamp to illuminate their evening sing-along.

Alfred about investing a large sum of money to expand the oil business. In 1879, the three brothers, with some other partners, formed the Nobel Brothers' Naphtha Production Company. Naphtha is similar to kerosene, and both come from oil. This company was known as Branobel. The oil business grew very rapidly.

Robert left Baku to go home to Sweden in 1880. He was not in good health, so he retired. Alfred mostly left the running of the oil company to Ludvig. In the 1880s, he helped out when it had problems. He went to St. Petersburg in 1883 because he thought Ludvig was spending too much money on expanding the business instead of on earning money. This kind of problem was common in business. The brothers

The 1870s World

By the 1870s Britain, Russia, Prussia, France, and Austro-Hungary had tremendous influence in the political world. The empires in Asia got smaller as the ones in Europe grew, especially Russia and Prussia. Russia and the United States had almost reached their largest sizes. Science and technology made leaps forward, leading to industrial growth. Building materials got better, so buildings and bridges got larger, machines were starting to be powered by electricity, and farm machinery made planting and harvesting easier. The lightbulb and telephone were invented. Oil's importance grew from being a light source to being a way to power all these new machines. Around the world, more people moved to cities to find work as industrialization spread. They wanted more rights and more say in their governments, so the push for constitutions grew stronger.

sometimes fought over how the company should be run. Ludvig wanted to expand the company with less caution than Alfred would have exercised. Alfred always wanted to exercise caution, especially because the amounts of money the company needed were huge. Overall, the oil company was a great success, producing vast quantities of oil.

The Nobel oil business in Baku became very large. They pumped oil out of the ground, then refined it into different products such as naphtha.

EXPLOSIVE BUSINESS

Nobel gave a lecture in London in 1875 in which he said, ". . . in a mine it is wanted to blast without propelling; in a gun to propel without blasting." He was talking about gunpowder, but he could have been defining the perfect industrial and military explosives. His blasting gelatin was said to be the "perfect explosive" for industrial uses. He then turned to making the perfect military explosive.

This new explosive needed to solve many problems. First, it shouldn't actually blast. Bullets are sent out of a gun barrel by a force that pushes them out. Too much force exploded all at once is less useful than a steady burn used to propel, or push forward, the bullet quickly. Second, the explosive needed to be smokeless. Smoke was a problem on the battlefield. Commanders couldn't give proper orders when it got too smoky for them to see the battlefield. The places from which gunmen fired were too easy for the enemy to see when smoke poured out of their guns. The guns themselves got gummed up from the smoky mess left behind by poor explosives, so they had to be laboriously cleaned and reloaded between firings.

It took Nobel until the 1880s to create ballistite, his perfect military explosive. Experts disagree on exactly when he invented it, but he first patented it in 1887. Ballistite is a mixture of nitrocellulose, such as guncotton, and nitroglycerin with a small amount of camphor added to it. Camphor is a gummy chemical that can make other materials more moldable. Ballistite is a moldable solid, so it can be made into whatever shape is needed. It is smokeless and leaves no residue behind to gum up gun barrels. It is easy and cheap to make and can be kept for a long time without going bad. Best of all, even though it is incredibly powerful, it doesn't actually explode. It burns quickly and with great heat, but very predictably. Experts thought it would change the way battles were fought, and it did.

The picture on the top shows soldiers firing guns using gunpowder. The smoke made battle difficult. On the bottom the guns were fired using Poudre B, which was much less smoky. Nobel's ballistite produced similar low smoke results.

NINE

A Traitor to France?

At the same time that Nobel was working on ballistite, a French chemist invented a different kind of almost smokeless military explosive. His name was Professor P. M. E. Vieille, and his powder was called Poudre B. The French government had already decided to use Poudre B for its army and navy. When Nobel offered to sell them ballistite, they turned him down. The Italian government was the first to buy Nobel's new product. It ordered 300 tons of it in 1889. Nobel was to be paid a fee for every kilogram made.

Even though France had refused to buy ballistite, it was not happy that Nobel had sold it to Italy. In 1881, Nobel had bought an estate northeast of Paris in Sevran. He had set up a bigger and better-equipped laboratory there than the one in his Paris mansion. The French government's own explosives research laboratory was near his at Sevran. Nobel was accused of having stolen ideas from it. The French newspapers started printing stories stating that Nobel was a spy and a traitor to France. He was no longer allowed to make ballistite or test guns at shooting ranges in France. His laboratory was broken into and searched by the French police.

Nobel was miserable about the way his good name and his private laboratory were being abused. He decided that he could no longer live and work in France. Although he kept his house in Paris and visited it fairly often, he decided to move to Italy. He bought a villa in San Remo in 1890. It was a beautiful home with a big yard that was like a park, and it overlooked the Mediterranean Sea. He named his new home Villa Nobel.

Meanwhile, in Paris in 1890, Paul Barbe, Nobel's French business partner, committed suicide. In 1886, Nobel and Barbe had joined all of Nobel's companies into two trusts. One was based in London and the other in Paris. When Barbe died, there was a great scandal. It turned out that he had been cheating the French government. He had also lost a lot of money for Nobel's French Dynamite Company.

At first Nobel thought he was bankrupt again. Luckily, the monetary losses weren't as bad as it seemed at first, and the companies recovered.

In the 1880s Nobel often complained about his poor health. However, as this photo shows, he looked well and strong.

However, all the years of running his businesses had worn Nobel out. He was tired of taking such responsibility for how they were run. Many businesses are governed by boards of directors. Nobel had been on most of his companies' boards. By 1891, Nobel gave up his places on all the boards. He decided to spend his energy on inventing instead. He kept ownership of large parts of the companies, but didn't help with their day-to-day operations anymore. However, he still stayed more involved than he would have liked. Even though he only took part in making important company decisions, there were still many of these to make. Alfred wrote to Robert, "I am totally sick and tired of the explosive-substance field, in which one is forever stumbling around in accidents, preventative clauses, red tape, acts of villainy, and other unpleasantness. I long for peace and quiet and want to devote my time to scientific experiments, which is not possible when every day brings new problems."

Nobel's lab at San Remo was fitted with the best equipment available. He spent a great deal of time experimenting there.

HEALTH AND FAMILY PROBLEMS

Nobel thought the move to sunny Italy might help improve his poor health. In December 1887, he wrote from Paris to Sofie Hess, ". . . .My hearing is beginning to go, I am depressed, and my digestion has never been worse. I feel that the old machinery will not work much longer; therefore I must work like a horse in order to get everything done." By this time, he had cut himself off from most socializing. He did what his businesses needed and experimented. Besides business partners and family members, Nobel saw very few people. He stopped eating out and traveled less often. Although he never had sounded cheerful in his letters, they began to sound even more depressed and lonely.

Beginning in 1885, Ludvig was often unwell. He had heart and lung problems. In 1887, he was diagnosed with tuberculosis. He retired, and his son Emanuel took over the Branobel oil business. On April 12, 1888, Ludvig died after suffering a heart attack. A huge funeral was held, and Ludvig was buried in St. Petersburg. Now there were just two Nobel brothers left.

In July 1888, Nobel wrote to Hess from Vienna, "Around two o'clock in the morning I suddenly became so sick that I had neither the strength to call anyone nor open the door. I was forced to spend several hours completely alone without knowing if they were my final ones." Nobel suffered from pains in his heart. He was only fifty-four years old, but he was sure he was close to death.

Nobel was always very close to his mother Andriette. Wherever he was, he sent her money, presents, and letters. He was always very loving toward her. Because they lived fairly far apart, he saw less of her than he would have liked. Andriette wrote at the end of 1888 to Alfred, "I have received everything through my Alfred's hardworking efforts. I own so much and can fulfill any of my wishes—except for two that cannot be bought for money: excellent health and to see my . . . darling as often as I would want." Andriette died not long after she wrote that, in 1889. He took the money she left to him and set up charities in her name. He also had a tombstone made with sculptures of Andriette, Immanuel, and Emil, who were all buried together in a family plot.

In September 1892, Alfred wrote to Robert from San Remo, ". . . I have been a frozen wretch my whole life, hardly able to stand a whiff of

Alfred Nobel enjoys a quiet moment in San Remo. He liked the climate and worked well there, but he also kept close ties to Sweden.

wind or rain. . . . My sensitivity to cold, and nothing else, has driven me to the shores of the Mediterranean Sea. . . . But the summers are so warm that even my paws thaw . . ." Coming from Alfred, this was high praise indeed.

TALKING ABOUT PEACE

Alfred Nobel said he hated war, but his work created explosives that were used for fighting. Each of his improvements made guns and cannon work even better. By 1885, he was growing more and more unhappy with how much people fought each other. He wrote to people who worked for peace stating that he feared an increase in war in the future. Nobel met with Bertha von Suttner and her husband Arthur in Paris in 1887. Their friendship began again. Bertha became a famous pacifist and wrote a book called *Lay Down Arms!* When Nobel read it in 1890 he was impressed. He began writing back and forth with Bertha, talking about peace and how to make it happen.

Nobel wrote to Bertha, "War is the horror of all horrors and the greatest of all crimes." He helped pay for the 1892 Peace Congress that was held in Bern, Switzerland. He went along, but without letting people know who he was. He wrote to Bertha, "Good intentions alone will not assure peace. . . . You must have an acceptable plan to lay before the governments."

Nobel talked with other people about his ideas for peace as well. Nobel did not think that peace meant weapons should be eliminated. He thought that countries needed to have weapons and armies so they could make the threat of war ensure that peace was kept. Long before nuclear bombs were invented, Nobel said, "War must be made as deadly to the civilian populations back home as it is for the troops on the front lines. . . . [This would mean that] all wars will be stopped instantly." In 1890, he wrote, "On the day when two armies will be able to annihilate each other in one second, all civilized nations will recoil from war in horror and disband their forces." In the twentieth century, both of these things became possible with nuclear and chemical weapons. War has not ended as a result.

One of Nobel's ideas was that countries should be forced to talk about their issues before they went to war. They should have to justify why they were going to fight. A group of countries would protect each other from attack by threatening to fight as a group against any party that attacked one of them. This is similar to the idea that started the United Nations, which does try to get countries to communicate to solve problems instead of going to war over them. If war is agreed to be necessary, the United Nations can work together to join many countries' forces into a large coalition that will fight against its target.

THE SPLIT FROM SOFIE

Nobel and Sofie Hess fought and made up many times over the years. Finally, in 1891, Hess left Nobel. She had a baby and married its father. Nobel still sent her money when she asked for it, saw her from time to time, and gave her money every year as an income. They kept writing letters to each other, mostly about money and the state of their health.

Clearly, Nobel and Hess valued their relationship. Perhaps Nobel needed someone to whom he could complain openly about his health, his business, his friends, and his family. He may have felt that all the money and worry that Hess cost him was worth it for this.

Hess never learned how to live on little money, and worried about keeping her daughter well and happy. Nobel almost always sent Hess the money she needed and made sure her family would not go bankrupt. Hess wrote to Nobel on July 10, 1894, "Even if love wears off with time, our warm friendship has to remain all the way to the grave. I also beg you to remain a good friend to my child, who's so dear to me." In his last letter to Hess on March 7, 1895, Nobel wrote, "When all is said and done, you are an emotional little creature and, after all, that is worth something."

TEN

Coming to an End

In 1893, Alfred Nobel turned sixty. He still read and wrote many letters, but his eyesight quickly got worse and he had a hard time seeing well enough to read. He wrote to his brother Robert in July, "Yesterday's mail contained 57 letters and 10 telegrams. I have no secretary, and it is difficult to get one for the kind of business I do." He also complained about his poor health and how he felt his life was soon going to end. Robert wrote to Alfred about his poor health and his worries about his four children. Alfred said that Robert had "an iron constitution compared to me." In reality, both were unwell.

Nobel started traveling back to Sweden more and decided to buy a manufacturing plant in Bofors. He wanted to make cannon there, enough "to see Sweden rival Germany and England when it comes to arms." He was working on improving the way guns fired. He also bought a house nearby called Björkborn Manor. Perhaps he was homesick for Sweden and wanted to see Robert and his family more often, or perhaps he felt Sweden would let him perform his gun experiments more freely than another country would. In 1893, Alfred Nobel was given an honorary doctor of philosophy degree by Uppsala University in Sweden. He was deeply honored by this award.

In 1893 Nobel met Ragnar Sohlman for the first time. Sohlman was a Swedish chemist and engineer who was only twenty-three years old. He was hired to be Nobel's secretary, but after three days on the job, Nobel decided he would be better used working in the laboratory. Sohlman worked in San Remo and later in Bofors. He and Nobel became close friends, possibly because Nobel saw a bit of himself

This photo was taken the year Nobel died. While he didn't look like an old or sick man, he did look more tired than in his earlier pictures.

as a young man in Sohlman. Sohlman was a gifted scientist, but also had the scope and ability to handle complicated matters, just as Nobel could.

Nobel was having problems getting permission to patent ballistite in England. The government was concerned that it was unstable. Nobel tried to solve the problem they pointed out. In the meantime, two British chemists, Sir Frederick Abel and Sir James Dewar, found a different way to make it more stable. They called their invention cordite. Nobel felt that it was too much like ballistite to be given a separate patent. The argument over the patent went to court and it took two years to resolve. In 1895, Nobel lost the case and had to pay a lot of money in legal fees. He was very angry about the loss, and felt that he had been wronged because of political deals.

Nobel Man

Ragnar Sohlman became one of Alfred Nobel's most trusted partners. Sohlman was much younger than Alfred. When he was a student, he traveled to Baku to meet with Robert Nobel. Then went on a long trek into the Caucasus, a mountain range. He wrote, "I was often asked where I came from, and this was difficult to explain, since the word schved—Swede—meant nothing to the country people. However, as soon as I mentioned that I came from the same country as Nobel, the comment was always the same: 'Oh, you are Nobelskij—a Nobel man.' To simplify matters, I finally adopted this title—little thinking that I was to become a Nobelskij for most of my life."

THE SIMPLE WILL

By 1895, Nobel had written the final draft of his will. It was very short. The important part is only one page long. Nobel wrote it out by hand and never had a lawyer check it over. He took it to the Swedish-Norwegian Club in Paris on November 27 and had four Swedish men sign it as witnesses. Perhaps Nobel thought this was a simple way to deal with the problem of distributing his fortune. However, the will ended up causing legal battles after his death.

Nobel's will gave certain amounts of money to his relatives and people who worked for him. He left Sofie Hess a yearly income. He left less money to his relatives than they were expecting. He wrote to Sofie in 1889, "I am taking great delight in advance all the widened eyes and curses the absence of money will cause."

Nobel was afraid of being buried alive. His father had had the same fear, which was common at the time. Nobel wrote in his will and in letters to friends and family exactly how he wanted his body to be treated after he died. He wanted to have doctors make sure he was dead. Then he wanted to be cremated, not buried.

Nobel had to name executors of his will. Executors are the people who make sure the will's wishes are carried out. One executor was Ragnar Sohlman. The other was a man Nobel had only met once or twice and had only known for six months. Rudolf Lilljequist was a Swedish engineer who worked with Nobel to create a new kind of chemical industry in Sweden. Nobel and Lilljequist had had a similar idea, and Nobel helped Lilljequist make it happen. Neither Sohlman nor Lilljequist had any idea they had been made executors until Nobel's will was read after his death.

This single page of Nobel's will caused all the tangled problems his executors had to resolve and made the plans for the Nobel Prizes.

The main part of Nobel's will caused most of the problems. It said that all of the rest of Nobel's fortune, which was about 31 million Swedish Crowns (about $155 million today), would be invested. The interest on it would be used to pay the winners of five prizes that would be given each year. The prizes would go to people who did things of the greatest benefit to human beings in five different fields: physics, chemistry, medicine, literature, and peace. Nobel named the groups who would decide on the prizewinners. Nobel's prizes were the first truly worldwide awards. He said that the winners could come from anywhere in the world.

On January 7, 1893, Nobel had written to Bertha von Suttner, "I would like to bequeath part of my fortune for the establishment of peace prizes to be awarded every fifth year . . . to the man or woman who has contributed most effectively to the realization of peace in Europe." Nobel thought that if peace wasn't achieved within thirty years, all of society would crumble. Nobel developed this idea into the will he wrote that set up the Nobel Prizes. Von Suttner helped him decide on the final wording. She was delighted that Nobel was using his money this way. She thought he was trying to help change the world because he believed in peace through the threat of awful destruction. Other people thought Nobel was trying to make his work on weapons and explosives look less morally wrong. They said he was trying to make himself feel less guilty about his work.

A GREAT MAN DIES

Ragnar Sohlman said that Nobel's last two years were more cheerful than his previous ones. He said that even though Nobel was not feeling well, he made new friends, worked on interesting projects, and bought new homes to keep him happy. Shortly before he died, Nobel was as busy as always. He had written a story called *Nemesis* and had arranged to publish it himself. He wrote a play about the lawsuit he had just lost in England. He was working on perfecting explosives and on improving guns. He also invented a camera that was strapped to a rocket that shot up into the air and took pictures of the land below. The pictures were useful for making maps. The camera came back down to earth gently on a parachute.

In September 1896, Alfred Nobel's brother Robert died in Sweden. By December, Alfred was feeling very ill. He asked for telegrams to be sent to his family and to Sohlman. He had been having attacks of chest pain because his heart was not getting enough oxygen. He was taking

NEMESIS

TRAGEDI I FYRA AKTER

Nobel wrote this story shortly before he died. It tells a lot about how he was thinking and feeling at the time.

nitroglycerin for this ailment, which opens up the blood vessels and lets more blood that is carrying oxygen get to the heart. This use of his explosive as a medicine amused him very much. On December 9, his condition grew worse. He had an Italian doctor and his servants to look after him. At the end of his life, he could only remember how to speak Swedish, and none of those comforting him understood it. At two o'clock in the morning on December 10, Nobel died after suffering a stroke.

Nobel's nephews, Emanuel and Hjalmar, and Sohlman all arrived in San Remo later that day. No one knew what Nobel's will said. On December 15, Sohlman found out that he was to be executor with Lilljequist, whom he had never met. When the will arrived on December 18, Sohlman said, "It had a depressing effect on all of us." There were problems because the trust to run the prizes was not yet set up. Some of the companies Nobel was closely involved with, such as Branobel, would be forced to change because of the will. Emanuel Nobel ran Branobel, and he was very worried, but wanted to carry out his uncle's wishes.

The three men organized a short funeral service in San Remo on December 17 that led by Nathan Söderblom, a Swedish priest who was living in Paris and was a friend of Nobel's. Then, Nobel's coffin was taken by train to Stockholm. A grand funeral was held on December 29 in the Great Church. Finally, Nobel's body was cremated as he had wanted.

ELEVEN

Dream and Reality

Ragnar Sohlman and Robert Lilljequist faced a lot of difficulties when carrying out Nobel's wishes. They had to figure out how to sell all of Nobel's company shares without ruining the value of the companies. Sohlman took on most of the duties of the executor because Lilljequist was busy in a remote part of Sweden and couldn't travel as easily. Sohlman had to create inventories of all the things Nobel owned in all his homes. He hired lawyers in each of the countries in which Nobel worked to help wind up the estate. He also had to set up the Nobel Foundation to invest and manage the prize money. Nobel had already chosen the groups to name the prizewinners, but Sohlman had to convince them to do so. This was difficult because there was no mention of paying the groups for their time and effort.

Many newspapers thought Nobel's will left a great legacy to the world. They said his vision of giving prizes to people all over the world would help humanity in general. There was also a great deal of criticism of Nobel's wishes. People thought only Swedes should get the prizes, or that the money should be shared among people in general instead of a few specific people. There was already tension between the governments of Sweden and Norway, and by asking the Norwegian government to help decide the recipients of the peace prize, Nobel had made it worse.

Nobel's relatives didn't agree with the terms of the will. Earlier versions of Nobel's will had left them more money and property. They did not get a lot from this final version. Some family members decided to argue that the will was illegal and took their case to court to try and prevent the will from being put into action. Nobel had never given up his Swedish citizenship, even though he really hadn't lived in the country since he was nine years old. Because he had a house in Sweden, Björkborn Manor, it was decided that he was a Swedish resident when he died. Therefore, the family's case went to court in Sweden.

Close to six months after Nobel's death, the Swedish government declared that the will was legal in May 1897. The Swedish attorney general, the highest-ranking lawyer in the country, said that the Swedish government would do all it could to carry out Nobel's wishes as quickly as possible. There were still problems, however. King Oscar II of Sweden talked with Emanuel about the will in February of 1898. He said, "Your uncle was talked into this by fanatics, womenfolk mostly. . . . It is your duty to your family to make sure that their interests are not jeopardized by your uncle's nonsensical ideas." Emanuel said that his family would stick to the wishes expressed in the will, and would not take money that "rightfully belonged to deserving scientists."

Finally, all the groups named in the will agreed to choose the prizewinners. Nobel's relatives agreed not to challenge the will anymore, in return for some money and a say in how the Nobel Foundation was to be set up. All the problems with selling Nobel's property and changing his shares in his companies into cash were sorted out. On June 29, 1900, the Nobel Foundation was set up. Even King Oscar II eventually decided that the Nobel Prizes were a good idea. Except for the first year, he handed the prizes to the winners every year until he died in 1907.

Why the Prizes?

No one knows exactly why Alfred Nobel decided to use his fortune to give out the Nobel Prizes. Many people have guessed at his reasons. In 1945, Albert Einstein said that Alfred Nobel "invented an explosive more powerful than any then known—an exceedingly effective means of destruction. To . . . relieve his conscience, he instituted his awards for the promotion of peace."

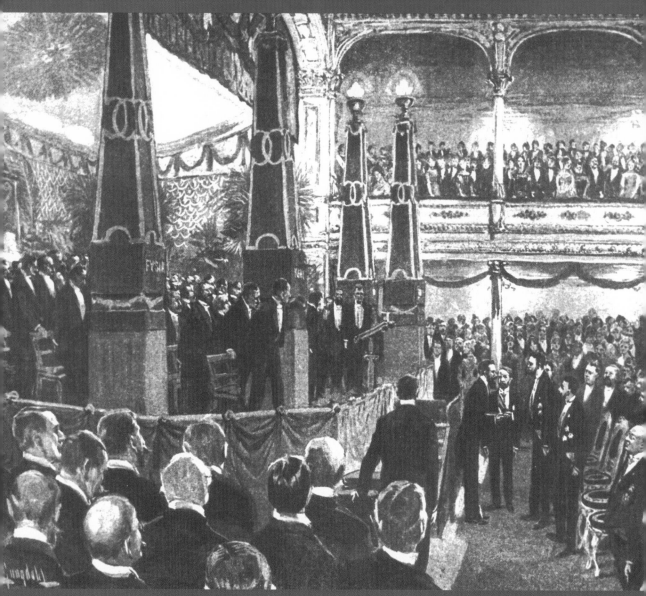

The first Nobel Prize ceremony was held in 1901. Hundreds of important people came to see the first laureates receive their honors.

THE NOBEL FOUNDATION

On September 27, 1900, the first board of directors of the Nobel Foundation was elected. The groups that chose the prizewinners also had members on the board of the foundation. The foundation exists to manage Nobel's fortune, to organize the prize award ceremonies, to tell people about the prizes and Nobel's life and works, and to make sure the groups that pick the prizewinners are looked after. It does not have anything to do with choosing the prizewinners themselves. Because Nobel said that the Norwegian government would help pick the Peace prizewinner, Norwegians are also represented in the Nobel Foundation. The Nobel Foundation is headquartered in Stockholm.

The first prizes were awarded in 1901 at a special ceremony in Stockholm. Since then many people have become Nobel laureates, as prizewinners are known. Sometimes, two or three people share one prize if they have worked together on an idea or if both of their works are so important that they split the award. Every October the winners are chosen. On December 10 of each year, the prizes are given out in a splendid ceremony. The Peace Prize is awarded at Oslo City Hall at the same time as the other prizes are awarded in Stockholm.

In 1965, the Nobel Foundation held its first symposium. A symposium is a meeting at which experts can share their ideas about a topic. There have been more than 120 of them since then.

In 1968, the Bank of Sweden gave money to the Nobel Foundation to fund a new prize for economics. Since then, the foundation has decided that no new prizes can be added. The foundation has been given

This is one of the rooms where the judges meet to review the nominees and decide on who should win the Nobel Prizes.

prizes itself. Many international groups have given money to the foundation because of how well it has handled the Nobel Prizes and how much good it has done as a result.

THE NOBEL PRIZES

Every year, the groups that choose the prizewinners ask famous and important people all over the world in the different fields to nominate winners. To nominate someone is to suggest the person to be the winner. The groups research all the nominees, and then winners are decided. Some years no prizewinners are picked in some of the categories. During World Wars I and II there were gaps in the prize awards. Because of the worldwide nature of the prizes, sometimes the laureates can't get to the award ceremony. Generally, all the prizes are given, and the laureates are there to receive them in person.

The king of Sweden hands out the prizes in physics, chemistry, medicine, literature, and economics. The Peace Prize is handed out by the chairman of the Norwegian Nobel Committee. Each laureate is handed a medal, a diploma, and a note saying how much money he or she will receive. Because the prize money is a share of the interest earned by the fortune Nobel left, the amount is different each year. In 2002, it was about $1 million for each prize. Each medal is made of gold. They all have a picture of Nobel on one side, but the other side shows something specific to the prize awarded. The diploma says who the laureate is, what the prize is, and the year. The group that picks the prizewinner chooses the diploma design. Most of the diplomas are works of art created by great artists.

In 2002, former President Jimmy Carter received the Nobel Peace Prize. He's on the left of this picture giving a speech to the people who came to see the ceremony.

Some of the best-known Nobel laureates are Marie Curie, who won two prizes, one in physics in 1903 and one in chemistry in 1911. Bertha von Suttner won the Peace Prize in 1905. Albert Einstein won the Physics Prize in 1921. The International Committee of the Red Cross has won the Peace Prize three times, in 1917, 1944, and 1963. Martin Luther King, Jr. won the Peace Prize in 1964, and UNICEF won it in 1965. In 1993, Nelson Mandela won the Peace Prize and Toni Morrison won the Literature Prize. President Jimmy Carter won the Peace Prize in 2002.

A GREAT LEGACY

Alfred Nobel changed many lives. His inventions changed industry and revolutionized the way the world looked. By making explosives more powerful, useful, and safer, he helped make it easier to build and mine. His work on military explosives changed how battles were fought. He was a man of vision and great ability.

Alfred Nobel also founded many companies. He had great skill in business. He knew how to get his inventions made and sold around the world. He ran complex companies in different countries, speaking different languages and traveling a great deal. He could discern how to make a company work and fix its problems with the same clear vision that helped him determine how to improve explosives.

Most important of all, Nobel was possibly the first to help people see the world as one international community instead of as separate countries. He succeeded in sharing his fortune with people doing great work in important fields. His prizes reward creativity and vision and make people talk worldwide about the work being done by the laureates. Although Alfred Nobel spent his life working on ways to blow things apart, his prizes truly bring people together by showing how much people are learning about the world and how people can work to make it a better, safer place to live.

Timeline

1868 Nobel patents dynamite in the United States on May 26.

Sweden bans the transport of nitroglycerin.

1869 Nitroglycerin Act bans the use of nitroglycerin in Britain.

1870 Nobel opens a dynamite factory in Paulilles, France.

1871 Nobel opens a dynamite factory in Ardeer, Scotland.

1872 Nobel's father, Immanuel Nobel, dies.

1873 Nobel moves to Paris.

Europe experiences an economic crisis.

1875 Nobel invents blasting gelatin at his house in Paris.

1876 Nobel meets Bertha Kinsky in Paris. Nobel meets Sofie Hess.

Alexander Graham Bell invents the telephone.

Thomas Alva Edison invents the electric light.

1879 Alfred, Ludvig, and Robert Nobel form The Naptha Production Company Brothers Nobel, known as Branobel, in Russia.

1886 Nobel works with Paul Barbe, his French partner, to consolidate all his dynamite companies into one trust.

1887 Nobel invents ballistite. France grants ballistite patent.

1888 Nobel's brother, Ludvig Nobel, dies of a heart attack in April.

1889 Nobel's mother, Andriette Nobel, dies.

The French government decides not to buy the rights to manufacture ballistite. The Italian government buys the rights instead.

1890 Nobel moves to San Remo, Italy, but keeps his house in Paris.

1891 Nobel and Sofie Hess split up.

1893 Nobel buys an arms manufacturing plant at Bofors, Sweden, and also the nearby Björkborn Manor. He is given an honorary doctorate degree from Uppsala University in Sweden.

1893–1895 The court case is fought over the similarities between ballistite and cordite in Britain, which Nobel loses.

1895 Nobel's will is signed by four Swedish witnesses at the Swedish-Norwegian Club in Paris on November 27.

1896 Nobel dies on December 10.

1897 Nobel's will is upheld by Swedish courts.

1900 Nobel Foundation is set up.

1901 First Nobel Prizes are awarded.

To Find Out More

BOOKS

McNair, Sylvia. *Sweden*. Danbury, CT: Children's Press, 1998.

Sachs, Jessica Snyder. *The Encyclopedia of Inventions*. Danbury, CT: Franklin Watts, 2001.

St. George, Judith. *So You Want To Be an Inventor?* Philomel Books, 2002.

Tesar, Jenny and Bryan Bunch. *The Blackbirch Encyclopedia of Science & Invention*. San Diego, CA: Blackbirch Press, 2001.

ORGANIZATIONS AND ONLINE SITES

Nobel Foundation
Box 5232
SE-102 45 Stockholm
Sweden

This organization oversees the assets that Nobel left in his will for the establishment of the Nobel Prizes.

The Nobel Museum
http:// www.nobel.se

This is the site for the Nobel e-Museum, which includes the Nobel Museum and the Nobel Foundation. It has the best collection of information about everything to do with Alfred Nobel, the Nobel Prizes, and the Nobel Laureates.

The Swedish Smorgasbord
http:// www.smorgasbord.se

Learn more about the culture of Nobel's homeland.

A Note on Sources

To research this book, I had to dig deep into the storage vaults of several library systems. Most of the books about Alfred Nobel's life were written a long time ago. Because he was Swedish, many of the books were written in Swedish and then translated into English. Most of them are now out of print, so they can be hard to find, but they are very interesting to read. I learned a great deal about explosives and how Alfred Nobel's discoveries changed the way the world works and looks.

Some of the books were written by people who knew and worked with Alfred Nobel. I found the information they gave me about what he was really like very useful. His own letters and writings are held by the Nobel Foundation. They give the best picture of what Nobel felt and did. The Nobel Foundation also has some of the things Nobel owned, such as his travelling bag. Seeing these things helped make his character more alive for me.

If you can find them, these books will help you learn more about Alfred Nobel. You can ask your local librarian for help if you want to start digging yourself!

I recommend: Kenne Fant's *Alfred Nobel: A Biography;* Tony Gray's *Champions of Peace: The Story of Alfred Nobel, the Peace Prize and the Laureates;* Ragnar Sohlman's *The Legacy of Alfred Nobel: The Story Behind the Nobel Prizes;* Trevor Williams's *Alfred Nobel: Pioneer of High Explosives.*

—*Tristan Boyer Binns*

Index

About the Author

Tristan Boyer Binns earned an English degree from Tufts University. She has written twenty-three books for children and young adults on subjects from the American flag to Fort Laramie to the CIA. She has taught creative writing to children and adults and has run writing workshops. Before beginning her writing career, Tristan was the publishing director for an international library book publisher. Researching people's lives is a real joy for her, especially when the facts are hard to uncover.

BPMS MEDIA CENTER